50
FOOTBALL
SKILLS

Gill Harvey, Jonathan Sheikh-Miller,
Richard Dungworth, Clive Gifford and Rob Lloyd Jones
Illustrations by Bob Bond
Photography by Chris Cole and Shaun Botterill
Designed by Tom Lalonde, Steve Wright and Neil Francis

Contents

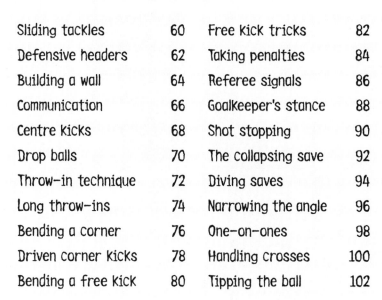

First touch

Controlling the ball as you receive it is one of the most important skills you can learn. A good first touch keeps the ball moving and places it a short distance from your feet.

Don't just hope the ball will come to you – move into line with it.

Here, the player is 'cushioning' the ball with his foot. This slows the ball down without making it bounce away.

Cushioning the ball

Cushioning the ball means taking the speed out of it, just as a cushion would if it were attached to your body.

1. As the ball travels towards you, position your foot in line to receive it.

2. On making contact, relax your foot and let it travel back with the ball.

3. The speed of the ball is absorbed. It slows down and you can play it away.

Foot control

A good first touch can slow the ball down and position it in one movement. If you use the inside of your foot, you will be in a good position to play the ball away when you have controlled it.

1. Watch the ball as it approaches and place your foot in line with it. Balance on one leg with your receiving foot turned out.

2. As you receive the ball with the inside of your foot, relax your leg and foot so that they travel back with it.

3. The ball should drop just in front of your feet.

Foot control exercise

Try this game with a friend. Make a 'gate' with two markers and stand with the gate between you. Pass the ball through the gate so that your partner has to control it.

He passes the ball down the outside of the gate. Control it, turn and pass it back through the gate or down the other side of it. Carry on passing and receiving like this.

The ball has been passed down the middle.

The player can now turn to the right or left.

The gate is about 2m (6ft) wide.

Try to vary your passes as much as possible, but keep them low.

Your pitch is about 5m (15ft) wide.

Juggling

Although you rarely need to use juggling in an actual game, it helps you to develop the quick reactions, tight ball control and concentration you need in order to play well.

To get the ball into the air, roll your foot back over the top of the ball, then hook it under and flick the ball up.

Keep the ball in the air by bouncing it off your foot. Hold your foot out flat. If you point your toes, you will probably lose control.

As you develop your control, pass from one foot to the other, or bounce it higher and juggle it off your knee, shoulder or head.

Juggling practice

Work on your juggling with a group of friends.
Choose someone to be a caller. All of you dribble until
the caller shouts 'Up!'

Now, everyone flicks the ball up and juggles. The last
one to keep the ball in the air wins. When he drops
it, you all start dribbling again.

Control heading

Controlling the ball with your head is not very easy until you are sure of your heading technique. But once you've got it right, it can be a great way to control high balls.

As the ball comes close, try to keep your eyes open. Stay relaxed right up to the last minute.

Use your forehead, not the top of the head.

Control heading technique

When practising this technique, you may find
it easier to begin with a softer ball.

1. As the ball approaches, stay
relaxed to provide a cushion.
Keep your eyes on the ball.

2. Hold your position as
you receive the ball. Bend
your knees and lean back
slightly further.

3. Push the ball forward
gently, so that it lands not
far from your feet.

Practice exercise...

With a partner, stand about 4m (12ft) apart from each
other. Your partner then throws the ball for you to
control. Let it drop to the ground, then pass it back.
Swap after five goes.

11

Using your chest

Your chest is good for controlling high balls because it's bigger than any other part of your body. Keep your arms out of the way, to avoid handling the ball.

1. Put your arms back and open up your chest as the ball approaches.

2. As the ball makes contact with you, cushion it by letting yourself relax.

3. Bring your shoulders in and hollow your chest, so that the ball rolls off you.

Chest control practice

Do this practice in pairs. One of you throws the ball to the other, as you would for a throw-in. The other person controls it with their chest and passes it back. Swap after ten throws.

Vary the angle and height of the throws.

Keep your hands open, which helps you relax.

Run into the best position to receive the ball.

Shielding the ball

Shielding is a way of keeping control of the ball by preventing other players from getting at it. You position yourself to become a shield between your opponent and the ball. This is also known as 'screening'.

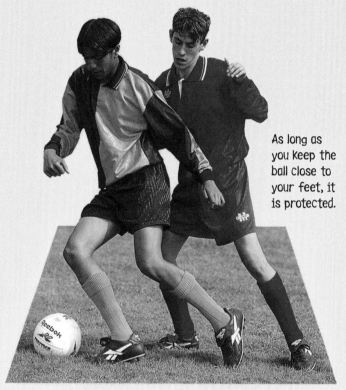

As long as you keep the ball close to your feet, it is protected.

As soon as you are challenged, turn so that you are between the ball and your opponent.

The challenger risks giving away a foul if he tries to kick the ball from behind.

Shielding when running

When you are running with the ball or dribbling, keep your head up to watch out for opponents coming up on your left or right side.

Be ready to change your body position from one side of the ball to the other.

For example, if someone is coming up on the right, keep the ball on your left side.

Dribbling

One of the most exciting parts of football is keeping the ball under control and dribbling it up the field.

You can use your instep to dribble, especially for the first few touches. Be careful not to kick the ball very far.

You are free to run faster if you use the outside of your foot, but try not to tap the ball too far out to the side.

The inside of your foot may feel the most comfortable to use.

Be careful not to let the ball get under your feet.

Dribbling practice

You need to be flexible and balanced to dribble well. To develop these skills, dribble around a course. Lay ten markers about 4m (13ft) apart in a zigzag line. Start to dribble down the line, weaving around the markers.

Keep the ball close to your feet. Try to exaggerate the twists and turns, leaning as far as you can as you run.

Keep as close to the path of the course as possible. Turn sharply at the markers.

In a game, you would need to look out for other players, so try to look around as you dribble.

Run lightly on your toes, so you can change direction quickly.

The stop move

If you are trying to lose your opponent while dribbling the ball, you stand a better chance if you know a few trick moves. The stop move is a good way of changing direction and unbalancing your opponent.

1. Accelerate slightly as your opponent is chasing you. As your opponent speeds up to follow, stop suddenly.

2. Drag the ball back and carry out the turn while your opponent is still off balance.

3. Finish the turn and move away at right angles to your original direction.

The stop-start game

The key to this move is speed. This game will help you develop the pace you need to throw your opponent off balance.

Work with a partner. Mark out a line about 20m (60ft) long. Dribble along it with your partner behind you.

Your partner can come alongside, but he cannot overtake you. Try to 'lose' him by stopping suddenly.

You may confuse him more if you pretend to stop, then accelerate. Keep the ball on the side furthest from him.

Feinting

Feinting means fooling your opponent while you are dribbling by using the movement of your body. This is also called 'selling a dummy'.

1. The simplest feint is pretending to go one way, then swerving and going the other. Here, Player 1 dribbles up the field as Player 2 comes to challenge him.

2. Player 1 drops his right shoulder, making Player 2 think that he is going to turn to the right.

3. Player 2 moves to the right, but Player 1 now swerves back to the left. He dodges around Player 2 and accelerates past him.

Feinting tips...

Good defenders will watch the ball, not your movements. Remember these tips when trying to sell them a dummy.

1. Exaggerate your dropped shoulder and body swerve to fool your opponent.

2. Accelerate past your opponent before he has time to recover.

3. Be confident when you try to sell a dummy, or you risk losing the ball.

Turning tricks

The drag-back turn

This trick is ideal if you are being closely marked and want to lose your opponent. Once you have mastered it, you can adapt it depending on your position.

1. Draw your leg back as if you are about to kick the ball, but swing your foot over it instead.

2. As you bring your leg back again, catch the top of the ball with your foot and drag it back.

3. As you drag back, begin to spin on your other foot. Lean in the direction you want to go.

4. When you have pulled the ball all the way back, complete the turn. Accelerate past your opponent.

The Cruyff turn

This turn was named after Dutch player Johan Cruyff.
Try to exaggerate the movements, or give the turn
extra disguise by pretending to kick the ball first.

As you're about to turn,
swing one foot around the
ball so that it's in front
of it. Keep this foot
firmly on the ground.

Leaning away from the
ball, push it back and then
behind you with the other
foot. Turn quickly
and follow the ball.

Watch where the
ball goes, so you
can follow.

Tricks with your heel...

The flick over

This trick is impressive, but don't use it in a game as it's likely you'll give the ball away. Learn it for fun, or compete with your friends to flick it the highest.

1. Step in front of the ball with one foot. Trap the ball between the toes of one foot and the heel of your other foot.

2. Roll the ball up your heel, then flick up backwards with your front foot as hard and high as you can so that it goes over you.

3. Try not to look round at the ball as you do the flick.

Tricks with your heel...

The heel catch

This is a fun trick to try while you are juggling.
Move in front of the ball, then lean forward and
flick your heel up to catch it.

The ball should come round to the front of you
again. Spin round to play it back into the air with
your instep or knee.

The push pass

This is a low kick for short distances. It's called a pass, but you can use it to shoot at close range. It's easy to learn, and accurate.

1. Swing your foot back, turning it out so that it is almost at right angles to your other foot.

2. Keep your ankle firm and your body over your feet. Make contact with the middle of the ball.

Kicking foot

Non-kicking foot

3. Follow through in a smooth, level movement. Keep your foot low – try not to sweep it upwards, as this will make the ball rise.

Push pass practice

Work with a friend. Place two markers 60cm (2ft)
apart. One of you stands 1m (3ft) in front of them,
the other 1m (3ft) behind. Try to pass to each other
through the gap. Score a point for each success.

2m
(6ft)

After five passes each, move another 1m (3ft) apart
and start again. Carry on until you are 10m (30ft) apart.
The player with the most points wins.

Wall passes

A wall pass, or 'one-two', is a great way of getting past a player while you are running at speed or dribbling the ball.

Just before your opponent challenges you, send a sideways pass to a team-mate. Sprint past your opponent as your team-mate knocks the ball back into your path.

The wall player needs to move into position at the very last moment, so that he loses his marker.

Don't pass the ball too soon or your opponent will be able to drop back and block the move.

Make sure both passes are fast enough to beat the defender, but not too difficult for the receiver to control.

Wall pass game

Mark out an area 24 x 6m (80 x 20ft) and divide it into four equal 'zones'. Five attackers and four defenders take up starting positions as shown.

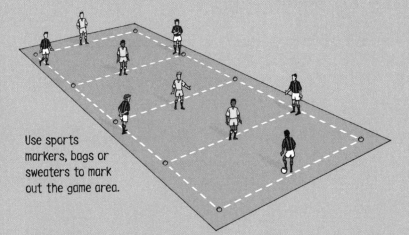

Use sports markers, bags or sweaters to mark out the game area.

The player with the ball tries to take it from one end to the other. He can dribble past a defender, or use a wall pass. He scores a point for each zone he crosses.

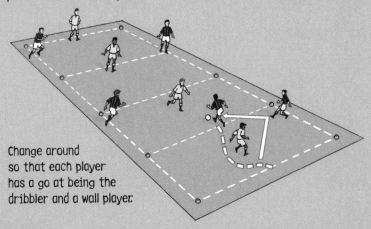

Change around so that each player has a go at being the dribbler and a wall player.

Crossing technique

If you've built an attack down the wing, you need to cross the ball back across the front of the opposition goal to give a team-mate the chance to shoot.

To hit a cross, you use the inside of your foot to strike through the lower half of the ball. Striking the ball slightly off-centre will make it spin, so that your cross swings into the target area.

Wrap your foot around the outside of the ball as you kick, to make it spin.

Swing your kicking leg across your body as you follow through.

Kick the lower half of the ball to make it rise.

Crossing practice

Place two markers as shown. Player A passes to player B, who dribbles along the wing. At the second marker, he crosses the ball to player C.

Vary the position of player C to practise different lengths of cross.

Move the second marker for crosses nearer to, or further from, the goal-line.

The players all move round one position, as shown, with player C taking the ball back to the first marker. The sequence then begins again.

You could add a defender whose job is to prevent player B getting in his cross.

The low instep drive

Your instep is the area over your laces. You can use this kick as you are running to send it a long way. It's quite difficult to make accurate, but the secret of success is to hit the ball right through the middle.

1. Swing your kicking leg well back, so that your heel almost reaches up to your behind.

2. Point your toes toward the ground and make contact with the middle of the ball.

Place your non-kicking foot close to the ball.

3. Swing your foot in the direction of the ball, but make sure your ankle is still stretched out towards the ground as you follow through. This is the key to keeping the kick low.

Toes

Non-kicking foot (alongside ball)

Instep pass game

Use this game to help develop your instep kicking technique. It's best with four people, but you could play with any number above two – change the shape of the pitch to make a corner for each player.

Mark out a 30m (90ft) square. Label yourselves A, B, C, and D and stand at its four corners.

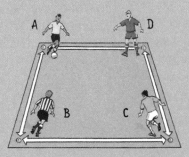

A passes to B at an angle so that he has to run on to it. B receives it and passes it at an angle to C.

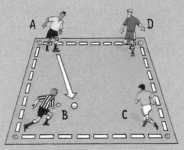

After passing, B stays where he is. C runs on to the ball and passes it to D, and so on around the square.

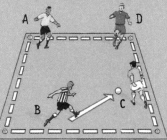

The lofted drive

The lofted drive is a long, high kick. The technique for doing it is similar to the low instep kick, but you need to kick the ball in a different place.

1. Approach the ball from a slight angle. Swing your leg back, looking down at the ball as you do so.

2. Make contact with the lower half of the ball, so that your instep reaches slightly under it.

Kicking the ball on its lower half makes it rise.

3. Follow through by letting your foot swing right up in a sweeping movement.

Lofted drive practice

With lofted drives, it's important to develop your technique. In this game you practise drives that need to be accurate as well as powerful to reach their target.

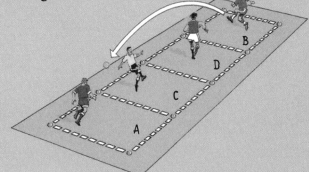

Four of you (A, B, C, D) can work at this by marking out a row of four boxes, all 10m (30ft) square. Each of you stands in a box, which you cannot move out of.

D intercepts the ball and takes the place of A.

A and B try to lob the ball over C and D. Score a point for each success. If C or D manages to intercept the ball, he takes the place of the player who kicked it.

Inside foot swerve

Swerving the ball is really useful when passing or shooting. You have more control with the inside of your foot than the outside, so it is best to learn the inside foot swerve.

1. With your eyes on the ball, swing your leg back. Keep your non-kicking foot out of the way of the ball.

2. Use the side of your foot to kick. The secret is to kick the ball in the right place (see below).

The ball should swerve out, then swing back in again.

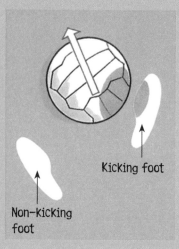

Kicking foot

Non-kicking foot

3. Follow through freely, your foot rising to follow the direction of the ball.

Pig in the middle

Play this game with two friends to practise your inside foot swerves. Stand in a line with 10m (30ft) between you. The player in the middle cannot move more than 60cm (2ft) to either side.

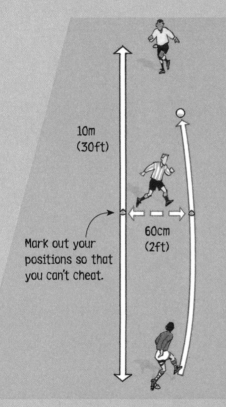

10m
(30ft)

60cm
(2ft)

Mark out your positions so that you can't cheat.

The players at each end try to bend the ball around the player in the middle using a foot swerve. If he is able to intercept it, the player who kicked it takes his place.

Outside foot swerve

This kick makes the ball swerve away to the side. You don't need to control the ball before you kick it.

1. As you swing your foot towards the ball, turn the toes of your kicking foot in slightly towards your other foot.

2. Kick the inside of the ball with the area around your little toe. Give the kick plenty of follow-through, sweeping your leg across your body.

3. The ball should swerve out away from you.

Non-kicking foot

Kicking foot

Pairs practice

Pass the ball down a straight line. Try to make it swing out from the line and back in again by using outside foot swerves.

Try standing further apart – 15m (45ft).

If you want an outside foot swerve to go higher, try using a lofted swerve kick. Kick the ball through its lower half and not through the middle.

Kicking foot swings under the ball.

The front volley

Front volleys are probably the easiest volleys to do, but you still need quick reactions for them. You use your instep to receive the ball, so you need to be facing it to keep the volley under control.

1. Lift your knees as the ball approaches. Point your toes and stretch out your ankle.

2. As you direct the ball away, try to keep your head forward over your knee.

Kick through the lower half of the ball.

The ball makes contact with your instep.

3. If you make contact later, your non-kicking foot should be closer to the ball.

Varying the height

If you want to send a volley high, get your foot right under the ball.

To stop the ball rising too much, lift your foot up over it slightly after making contact.

Learning to volley

Work with a friend. Stand 3m (10ft) apart. Drop the ball onto your foot and volley it for him to catch.

3m (10ft)

Side volley

You need quick reactions for side volleys, but the leg movement you have to do is also quite tricky — you need to be able to balance on one leg while you are leaning sideways.

1. Lean away from the ball, and swing your kicking leg up and around to your side.

2. Strike the ball with your instep. Hit it just above centre to keep your shot low.

3. Follow through by swinging your kicking leg right across your body.

Side action practice...

Make or find something that is almost as high as your hip, and try swinging your leg over it. You can put the ball on top of it if you want.

Trio volley game

When you can do the leg movement, play with two friends. A throws the ball to B, who volleys to C. C throws the ball for A to volley, and so on.

Score a point each time you volley accurately. The player with the most points after ten volleys each is the winner.

Shooting to score

To maximise your chance of scoring, you need to pick the most vulnerable part of the goal, and the best approach to beat the goalkeeper.

Always try to keep your shot low. This will be far harder for a goalkeeper to reach.

Aim just inside whichever post is furthest away from the goalkeeper.

Accuracy is more important than power – carefully placing the ball is better than blasting it wildly at goal.

Follow your shot in. If it rebounds from the goalkeeper, post or crossbar, you may get another chance to score.

Target practice

You can practise your aim by marking a target on a wall to shoot at, but it's even better to practise against a goalkeeper. This exercise is for five players.

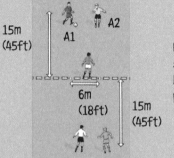

15m
(45ft)

A2

A1

6m
(18ft)

15m
(45ft)

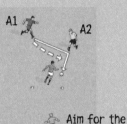

A1

A2

Keep the shots as low as possible.

Aim for the corners of the goal.

Mark out a goal 6m (18ft) wide. Stand in pairs, 15m (45ft) in front and behind the goalkeeper.

A1 passes to A2, who tries to shoot. A1 becomes a defender and tries to stop him.

A1

A2

B1

B2

The ball now goes across to the B players who follow the same pattern. B2 tries to score.

Next, swap around as shown and play until everyone has had ten shots. The best score of ten wins.

Heading in attack

To reach a low ball passing slightly ahead of you,
a diving header may be your only shooting option.
Approach this shot with courage and commitment.

1. Launch yourself at
the ball to give your
header power.

Direct the ball by
turning your
head as you
hit it.

2. Use your
forehead to drive
the ball forwards and
down into the goalmouth.

3. Break your fall with
your arms. Quickly get
back into play.

Heading practice

This is an exercise for three players. Mark out a goal 6m (18ft) across. Place a marker 15m (45ft) in front of it. One player is the goalkeeper.

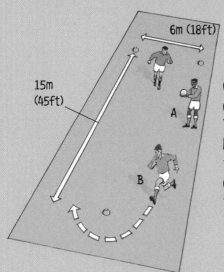

One player (A) stands at the side of the goal. The other (B) stands between the goal and the marker. B runs around the marker as A throws the ball to him.

B has to dash for the ball and try a diving header at the goal. Rotate players after ten goes.

Count how many times you can score.

Beating the keeper

As you approach the goal to shoot, the goalkeeper will often try to reduce the area you can aim at by moving out towards you. If you think he is likely to block a shot to either side, try dribbling the ball past him instead.

You need to make the goalkeeper commit himself. Make as though to shoot past him so that he 'spreads' to block the ball.

Once he is on the ground, take the ball past him, or chip it over him. Run on and aim the ball carefully into the goal.

Chipping the keeper

Another way to beat the keeper if he approaches you is to chip the ball over his head, so that it drops down into the goal.

Even if the goalkeeper jumps at the right time, he'll not be able to reach this high chip over his head.

For a chip, kick the bottom of the ball with a sharp, stabbing action.

Chipping

The chip is a kick which makes the ball rise very quickly into the air. It's ideal for lifting the ball over opponents' heads, especially the goalkeeper's.

1. Face the ball straight on. It is almost impossible to chip from the side. Take a short backswing.

2. Bring your foot down with a sharp stabbing action, aiming your foot at the bottom of the ball.

Direction of ball

Kicking foot

3. Your foot kicks into the ground as it hits the ball, which is why there is no follow-through.

Chipping practice

It is probably easiest to chip the ball as it is moving towards you. This exercise allows you to practise your basic technique with the ball coming towards you.

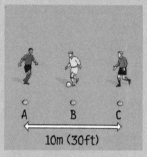

The exercise is for three players. Lay out three markers 10m (30ft) apart.

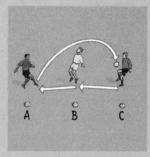

If A or B mis-hits a chip, he goes into the middle and C takes his place.

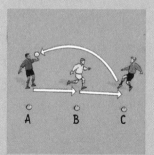

C plays the ball along the ground to B, who chips it to A. A passes it to C.

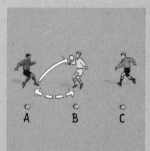

C passes along the ground to A. A chips it over C to B, who plays it back to C.

The overhead kick

The mark of a good striker is the ability to create goals from half-chances. This acrobatic technique means you can shoot from a cross even if you have your back to goal.

1. Watch the ball as it approaches. Lift your non-kicking leg and lean back.

2. To reach the ball, take off from your kicking leg, lying back as you jump.

3. Whip your kicking leg up and over to strike the ball with your instep. Put out your arms to break your fall. As you land, roll onto your shoulder.

Practising overhead kicks

Practise on soft grass or a cushioned mat. Get a friend to help you and stand about 5m (15ft) apart. Your friend throws the ball to you to kick.

At first, work on landing safely. Once you are sure about this, work on timing your jump, because timing is the main secret of success.

If the ball is thrown further away from you, try the 'scissors kick'. For this, you jump and kick while you are sideways in the air.

Jockeying

Jockeying means delaying your opponent's attack by getting in his way. This allows your team-mates to get into a position where they can help you to challenge.

Don't close in on your opponent too quickly. Otherwise, he will be able to judge your run and dodge round you easily.

Watch the ball carefully.

Direction of goal

Keep your weight on your knees, so you're in a strong position to challenge.

Once you are close to the attacker, hold off slightly. You should be close enough to touch him, but if you get much closer it will be easy for him to dash round you.

Maintaining the pressure

As well as delaying your opponent, try to force him into a weaker position. First of all, try to work out which is his weaker side – if he usually uses his right foot to dribble or kick, he is weak on his left side.

This player jockeys on the left.

Cover your opponent to the front and to one side so that it is difficult for him to turn.

The attacker is forced into the side-lines.

If you jockey on his strong side, he will only be able to use his weak side, so he may make a mistake.

Here, the attacker loses the initiative.

Once you have your opponent under pressure, watch for opportunities to win the ball.

Intercepting

The most direct way to win a ball off an opponent is to tackle, but this is not always the best. If you can intercept the ball, it will leave you with more control.

Approach your opponent at an angle. Don't get in too close to him, as he may be able to dodge around you. Always get into a goal-side position.

If you approach in this direction, you will be able to challenge the attacker.

Direction of goal

Wait for a chance to intercept. Attackers may make mistakes under pressure.

Intercepting exercise

This exercise helps develop your agility and speed at intercepting. Play in threes (A, B and C). Mark out a 10m (30ft) square. A and C stand in the middle, B along one edge. The direction of play is towards A and C.

C stands goal-side of A. B passes towards them. C must judge whether to intercept or stay goal-side.

If A gets the ball, C tries to stop him reaching the far side of the square before B can count to ten.

B scores a point if he stops A

If C intercepts, he scores a point and passes the ball back to B before A can challenge him.

A scores a point for turning and reaching the other side. After five goes, swap your roles around.

Front block tackles

To tackle well you need a good combination of good technique and plenty of determination. You need to tackle cleanly to avoid giving away possession of the ball, too.

If you watch your opponent instead of the ball, you may be tricked by a feinting move.

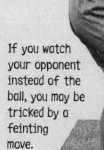

Watch the ball, not your opponent. With your weight forward, go into the tackle with your whole body.

Use the inside of your tackling foot to make contact with the middle of the ball.

Block tackle practice

In pairs, mark out a 10m (30ft) line. Start at each end. One player dribbles, the other challenges.

The dribbler tries to get to the end of the line, while the challenger tries to win the ball from him. Whoever succeeds scores a point.

10m (30ft)

Tackling from other angles...

You can use a block tackle to challenge from the side, but not from behind as this is a foul.

To tackle, turn your whole body towards your opponent so that your strength is behind the tackle. Use the side of your tackling foot. Lean into your opponent, but don't push.

Sliding tackles

Sliding tackles are a last resort. You should only use them in a real emergency. You'll probably not gain possession of the ball, and may give away a foul.

Approach from the side. Keep your eyes on the ball and slide your tackling leg forward to push the ball as far as possible.

After tackling, get up quickly. This is easier if you tackle with the leg furthest from your opponent.

Keeping it clean...

To avoid fouling in a slide tackle, remember these tips:

- Be patient. If you wait for the right moment to tackle, you are more likely to do so cleanly.
- If you kick the ball and not your opponent, you will not be penalised if he has to jump over you.

Learning to slide tackle

It's best to practise sliding tackles without an
opponent, so you're less likely to hurt someone.
Try this game with a friend.

Place two obstacles 5m (15ft) apart
and put the ball close to one of
them. These are your 'opponents'.
You both start next to
an obstacle.

Score a point each
time you tackle without
touching the obstacle.

One of you
runs up and
slides the ball
away, trying
not to touch
the obstacle.
The other
collects the
ball and puts it
next to his own
obstacle. He
slides it back.

Defensive headers

The penalty area is often crowded, so clashes with attackers in the air are bound to happen. Attacking the ball aggressively actually gives you greater control.

Communicate with your goalkeeper and team-mates to avoid clashing with them as well as with attackers.

Try to jump before the attacker. He may then push you up further from underneath.

Be careful not to give away a free kick. Don't push the attacker with your arms.

Header technique

In the defending third, and even more so in the penalty area, you need speed, courage and aggression to clear the ball out of danger.

As for any header, keep your mouth shut and your eyes open.

1. Take the ball as early as possible. Brace your legs and take off on one leg, springing at the ball and arching your back in the air.

2. Aim to hit the ball from underneath so that your forehead sends it high over attackers' heads.

3. If you need to, turn your head as you make contact to send the ball away from the penalty area.

Building a wall

A direct free kick allows opponents a direct shot at goal. You need a defensive wall to cover as much of the goal as possible without blocking the goalkeeper's view. The wall must be 9m (30ft) from the kick.

The tallest player stands in front of the post furthest from the goalkeeper.

Watch the ball by lifting your eyes, not your head.

You must form the wall quickly.

Everyone in the wall should stand very close to the player next to him so that there aren't any gaps.

Protect your head by tucking it down on your chest, and place your hands over your groin.

Positioning the wall...

...for central kicks

Line up so that the goalkeeper has a view of the ball.

Other players should mark attackers man-to-man.

The wall must hold firm as the kick is taken, then move quickly to follow up any rebounds.

...for kicks from the side

If the kick is to the side of the goal, it is more likely that the kicker will try to cross the ball to another attacker.

Here, you only need two or three players in the wall.

As soon as the kick is taken, move quickly to clear the ball out of danger.

Communication

Communicating with your team on the pitch is essential. Many defensive mix-ups and breakdowns in attack are due to a lack of communication. Here are some common calls on a soccer pitch.

'Man-On!' – tells the on-ball player that an opponent is approaching. Adding which side the player is coming from is even more helpful.

'Time' – tells a player about to receive or on the ball that he is unmarked and has space to turn and view the situation.

'Leave' or 'Mine' – tells a team-mate that you will take the ball.

'Force him outside' – is a defensive order meaning stay inside the attacker forcing him towards the touchline.

Communication practice

This fun game helps communication skills. A team of two players acts as defenders. They must try to get the ball from the team of five. Always try to use your team-mate's name when shouting 'leave', 'mine', 'time' or 'man-on'. Calls should be clear and calm.

The two defenders try to intercept the ball or make a tackle.

10m x 20m
(33ft x 66ft)
rectangle

Each player can only touch the ball three times in a row.

Members of the team with the ball are numbered from one to five. One can only pass to two, two to three and so on. If player five manages to pass to player one, the team scores a point. Swap the defenders over once the side has scored three points.

Centre kicks

All centre kicks are taken from the centre spot. Once you've struck the ball, you musn't kick it again until it's been touched by another player.

To keep possession, use a short pass to a team-mate standing alongside you in the centre circle.

Make sure the ball crosses the halfway line completely.

Use the inside of your foot to tap the ball forward gently into the path of your team-mate.

Your team-mate can quickly pass the ball to one of your team's players.

Creating an overload.

You can use a longer centre kick to move play upfield quickly and put pressure on the other team.

If you decide to try a long centre kick, your team will have a better chance of winning the ball if several of your players gather on one side of the pitch.

Angle your kick
to the "overloaded" side of the
pitch, into the path of your attacking players.

If the other team realizes what you are planning, try switching your centre kick move at the last minute, playing the ball to the other side.

Drop balls

A drop ball is used to restart play after a stoppage for which neither team is responsible, such as an injury. It gives teams an equal chance of gaining the ball.

The referee brings the ball back into play by dropping it onto the pitch between one player from each team. Neither player is allowed to play the ball before it hits the ground.

Concentrate on the ball. Try to get your foot to it as soon as it lands.

If your opponents had the ball when the game was interrupted by injury, it is good sportsmanship to let them win it back deliberately.

Winning drop balls

To win a drop ball you'll need sharp reactions and quick thinking. Keep your eye on the ball.

The simplest approach to a drop ball is to use the inside of your foot to tap the ball to a team-mate on your non-kicking side.

If you think your opponent will block an inside foot pass, try using the outside of your foot to hook the ball away to the other side.

You can even try pushing the ball forwards through the gap between your opponent's legs. Dart past him to collect the ball.

Throw-in technique

If an opposition player knocks the ball over either touchline, one of your team's players has to throw it back onto the pitch. This is known as taking a throw-in.

As you release the ball, part of both of your feet must be touching the ground, on or behind the touchline.

You cannot score a goal by throwing the ball straight into the opposition's goal.

Make sure that you hold the ball with your fingers spread around its back and sides. This lets you control it more easily as you release your throw.

Feet on ground, on or behind touchline

Practising throw-ins

For throw-ins, you need to be able to throw accurately or you may give the ball away. To improve your throw, try this exercise with a partner.

Stand about 10m (33ft) apart. Use throw-ins to pass the ball back and forth. Throw the ball to your partner's feet so they can control it easily.

As you get better at throwing the ball, your partner can give you a specific target area. Try throwing to your partner's head, chest and thigh.

Long throw-ins

Most teams have at least one player who specializes in throwing the ball a long way. Practise the technique here to develop a long, accurate throw-in.

1. Hold the ball in front of your head and take a couple of quick steps towards the touchline.

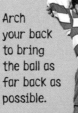

Arch your back to bring the ball as far back as possible.

2. Take a long final stride to reach the line, bringing the ball right back behind your head.

Place your leading foot close behind the touchline.

At least part of your trailing foot must be touching the ground.

Leading leg

3. With the weight on your leading leg, whip the upper part of your body forwards to catapult the ball away.

Feet on ground, on or behind touchline

Foul throws...

If you break one of the rules when you take a throw-in, the referee will ask the other team to retake the throw. The pictures below show how you could end up throwing away possession.

X FOUL THROW – The player's feet are too far over the touchline for a legal throw-in.

X FOUL THROW – The thrower's right foot is off the ground as he releases the ball.

X FOUL THROW – The player hasn't brought the ball far enough back over his head.

Bending a corner

You can make a corner even more effective by bending it, so that the ball swings towards the goal. Do this by striking the ball off-centre so that it spins as it travels through the air.

Hit the ball with the part of your foot around your big toe.

Lean back as you kick.

Approach the ball from a slight angle.

This view, from behind the ball, shows where you should strike it.

Get your non-kicking foot behind and to the side of the ball.

Who takes the corner?

Bending a kick using the inside of your foot makes the ball swing to the left if you're right-footed, or to the right if you're left-footed. You need to place the ball in the corner circle, so that you can kick it without the flag blocking your run up or swing.

Here, the ball is placed correctly for a right-footed corner kicker.

Here, the ball is placed correctly for a left-footed corner kicker.

A right-footed player bends corners in from right of the goal.

A left-footed player bends corners out from right of the goal.

Driven corner kicks

When you hit a swinging cross, the ball takes a long time to reach the goal area because it curves through the air. By striking a straight, powerful cross, you can send the ball across the goalmouth more quickly.

1. As you run up, get your non-kicking foot right up alongside the ball. Keep your body over the ball.

2. With your knee over the ball, and your toes pointing down, strike the ball just below its centre with the instep of your foot.

3. Follow through with your kicking leg to power the ball across into the penalty area. It will travel in a straight line, rising slightly.

Driven corner moves

Try to send a driven corner either to a player on the near side of the goal area, or one around the middle of the penalty area. A driven cross will stay low, so the receiver must be prepared to strike a waist-high volley, or even try a diving header.

Here, you can see an example of both a long and short driven corner move.

This player is acting as a decoy to create space in the middle of the penalty area.

This player is acting as a decoy to make space in front of the near post.

Signalling the move...

When you've decided what kind of corner move to use, signal to your team-mates so they know what you're planning to do. For this, you'll need to agree on a system of corner kick signals during training.

Bending a free kick

When you take a free kick near the penalty area, your opponents will usually protect their goalmouth by forming a defensive wall. To score, you need to get the ball past this wall of players.

Here, a right-footed player bends a free kick around the wall.

The player hits this red area of the ball with the inside of his foot.

Here, the right-footed player bends a shot in the other direction.

The player hits this red area of the ball with the outside of his foot.

Bending shot practice

To practise your swerving shot, put one corner
flag in the centre of the goal, and another on the
penalty spot. Place the ball on the penalty arc, in
line with the flags.

Try to bend a kick around one side of the nearest
flag into the other side of the goalmouth. Once
you've mastered that, place the ball further round
the arc so that you have to bend your kick more.

Training tips...

* Don't hit the ball too low or it will rise over
  the goal.
* Keep your toes of your kicking foot pointed
  down as you kick.

Free kick tricks

The back pass switch

You're unlikely to score from a free kick unless you create an element of surprise. Try this trick to switch the direction of an indirect free kick attack.

Approach the ball as though to kick to a team-mate on one side. Instead, roll it backwards to a player on the other side to shoot.

Use the underside of your foot to roll the ball to a team-mate behind you.

Free kick tricks

Dummy cross-overs

You can use this tactic to disguise the direction of a direct free kick shot.

1. You and a team-mate both prepare as though to take the kick.

2. Your team-mate runs up to the ball, as though to shoot, but steps over it at the last minute.

3. Time your own run up so that just after your team-mate "dummies" over the ball, you hit a powerful shot at goal. Your team-mate's run will help to hide your shot.

Taking penalties

When you take a penalty, don't be indecisive or hesitant. Pick your target area and concentrate on hitting a hard, low shot into that part of the goal.

Use your arms for balance.

Strike the ball through its midline, so that it stays low.

Follow through with your kicking leg for maximum power.

Approaching the penalty

Make sure you place the ball on the penalty spot yourself. That way you'll know it's on a sound surface.

1. The key to a low, hard shot is to keep your body over the ball as you kick, rather than leaning back.

2. Get your non-kicking foot alongside the ball so that the knee of your kicking leg is over the ball.

3. With your toes pointed down, use the instep of your kicking foot to drive the ball forward.

You may find it easier to place your shot accurately by hitting the ball with slightly less power, using the inside of your foot.

Referee signals

In the noise of a big game, it's not always possible to hear what the referee is saying, so it's useful to know the signals they use on the pitch.

Hand ball foul

Awarded for deliberate hand or arm contact

Stand back ten yards

For the opposition team at a free kick

Play on

The referee lets the play continue

Indirect free kick

Given for obstruction

More referee signals

Remember, the referee is in charge of the game. Don't argue with him – it doesn't help your team, and may earn you a yellow card.

Kicking foul

Player deliberately kicked

Pushing foul

Player pushed off ball

Foul throw-in

Feet over side-line

Tripping foul

Player deliberately tripped

Goalkeeper's stance

When you're waiting to make a save, you should stand in a position that allows you to react quickly. This is the typical stance used by goalkeepers. It shows you are alert and ready.

Keep your head still and your eyes on the ball.

Try to lean forwards slightly so you are ready to make quick and sudden falls or jumps.

Your hands should be at around waist height, with palms facing outwards.

Your legs should be slightly bent, and about a shoulder-width apart.

Your weight should be equally balanced on the balls of your feet.

Catching the ball

For shots that come towards you at chest or head height, the best catching technique is the W shape.

The palms of your hands face outwards and your index fingers and thumbs form a 'W' around the back of the ball.

Keep your eyes on the ball. If you look away, this could mean a dropped catch.

Catching practice

Lay out a zigzag pattern of markers with a gap of about 2m (6ft) between each one.

Weave through the markers, staying in the set stance as a team-mate throws shots at chest or head height.

Shot stopping

Scooping, or 'cradling', the ball into your body, is the safest way to catch a ball at waist or stomach height.

As the shot arrives, angle your hands downwards, giving the ball a clear path to travel into your body.

As the ball comes into contact with your chest or stomach, wrap your hands around it. Your body will cushion the shot.

Useful tips...

- Always try to lean into a shot. This makes it easier to scoop the ball into your body.
- You may need to take a small jump to get your body behind a slightly higher shot.

Shot stopping - barrier position

The barrier is the safe method for stopping ground level shots. Only use this when you have a clear view of the ball.

Place one knee on the ground, as shown in the picture. Put the foot of your other leg lengthwise alongside it, so that you make a long barrier.

Your hands should cover any gap between your foot and knee.

Your leg and foot provide extra protection behind your hands.

The bending scoop

With faster ground shots, it's better to use the bending scoop. As the shot approaches, bring your feet close together. Then bend down and scoop the ball into your hands.

It's risky to use this method on uneven playing surfaces. A deflection of the ball can cause problems.

The collapsing save

When you need to get down to the ball as fast as possible, falling to the ground is the best solution. Move quickly and collapse onto the shot.

1. Swing your legs to one side and drop down to the ball hands first. Your body will act as a barrier behind your hands.

2. Put both hands on the ball. One hand wraps around the back, while the other is on top. The wrapping hand acts as a barrier. The hand on top grips the ball to your body.

3. Once the shot has been stopped, pull the ball in close to your chest. Then curl yourself around the ball to help protect your body in a crowded goal area.

Collapsing practice

Mark out a goal about 4m (13ft) wide within the goal area. Place two more markers the same distance apart, about 3m (10ft) out from goal. Do the same again about 6m (20ft) out.

Ask a team-mate to stand on a line level with either set of markers and take shots at goal. Swap with your team-mate when you feel tired. Use your hands to save whenever possible.

Collapsing tips...

* You should practise collapsing saves regularly, because many keepers find them difficult to do.

* Don't overdo your collapsing movement. It shouldn't involve any acrobatic leaps.

This keeper didn't move fast enough.

* The ball will be moving fast, so get your hands down in time, otherwise the ball will squeeze under your body.

Diving saves

When attackers fire wide shots at goal, you'll need
to attempt a diving save. For this, the right jumping
and landing techniques are essential.

1. Just before you
are about to dive,
transfer your weight
onto the foot nearest
the incoming ball.
Push down hard on this
foot and then leap up.

2. As you leap, keep
your eyes on the
ball and dive slightly
forwards to attack
the shot.

3. Grasp the ball
tightly so that it
doesn't bounce out
of your hands when
you land.

Preparing for diving saves

Diving saves involve a lot of falling on the ground. Here are two games to give you more practice in this.

1. With a friend, stand a short distance apart from one another. Your team-mate then rolls the ball through your legs.

Turn around quickly and fall on the ball before it is out of your reach. Keep your body relaxed as you land.

2. Your team-mate throws balls a metre (3ft) either side of you. Crouch down to catch them, falling on your side as you catch.

Try to land on your side to help cushion your body.

Narrowing the angle

In goalkeeping, good positioning involves skilful footwork and getting your body behind the ball. This makes saves easier for you, and shooting harder for your opponents.

Here the keeper is out of position. He has left both sides of the goal wide open, giving the striker a clear view of the goal.

By coming off the goal-line, keepers reduce the view of the goal for attackers and 'narrow' the shooting angle. Shots become much easier for the keeper to reach.

The striker has a small target area.

The angles game

This game helps you practise getting in line with play and narrowing shooting angles. Ask two team-mates, each with a ball, to stand on either side of the penalty area about 14m (46ft) out from goal.

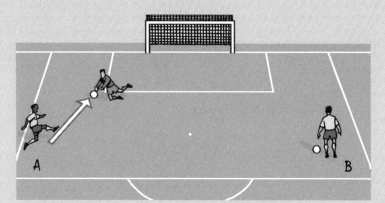

Get into line, shout 'ready' and then save from player A.

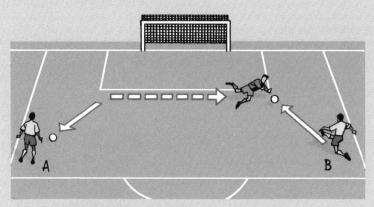

Do the same with player B. A and B should vary their positions before each shot.

One-on-ones

In 'one-on-one' situations against a striker, try to force the attacker wide, away from goal. This will make it more difficult for him to shoot and will give defenders a chance to get back and support you.

1. As the striker is running onto a pass but has not yet touched the ball, get quickly off your line and narrow the shooting angle.

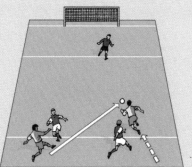

2. Once the striker has the ball, slow down, and watch out for a shot. Get into the set stance and block the route to goal.

3. As the striker tries to take the ball around you, stay in line and force him wide. It's now much harder for him to score.

Diving at an attacker's feet

When a striker attempts to dribble the ball around you, try to gain possession by diving at the player's feet.

Make your move when the ball is slightly ahead of the attacker and not totally under control. Only dive if you feel sure you will win possession.

Keeping your hands in front of your face to protect your head.

As you dive at an attacker's feet, try to 'spread yourself', making a barrier between the ball and the goal.

Once you have claimed the ball, wrap your body around it for extra security.

Handling crosses

Many goals come from high crosses aimed deep into the penalty area. Catch a cross if you can, but punch or tip if you have to. You need to be positive and go for the ball.

If you can make a clean catch, then clearly shout 'Keeper's ball!' as you take a running jump for it.

Jump off one leg and catch the ball about 30cm (1ft) in front of your face.

Lift up the leg nearest to the opposition to protect your lower body against challenges.

As you jump, turn sideways on to the opposition and face the ball. Try to catch a cross when the ball is at its highest point. This makes it harder for strikers to get up and reach the ball.

Punching crosses

If you're under so much pressure that you are unable to catch the ball, try to punch it away instead. A good punched clearance needs height and distance to give you enough time to recover your position if the ball goes straight to an opponent.

Take a running jump at the ball and shout 'Keeper's ball!'

To get maximum power in your punches, keep your fists together. Strike the ball firmly with the part of your hands between the knuckles and the finger joints.

If you can't get two hands to the ball, you may have to use a less powerful one-handed punch.

Tipping the ball

You should aim to catch most diving saves, but if a shot is too powerful or too well-placed to catch, a slight deflection, or tip, of the ball can be enough to push it off target.

When the shot touches your hand, make sure your palm is open and your fingers are spread wide. Try to push or flick the ball away.

Use only one hand to deflect the ball.

Keeping your palm open makes a bigger target for the ball to hit.

When you deflect the ball away, try to tip it over the bar or around the post.

Tipping overhead chips

If you are caught out of position, an attacker may chip the ball over you. As chip shots travel slowly, you have the chance to recover your position and tip the ball over the bar.

To practise this, place a marker 6m (20ft) from the centre of the goal and ask a team-mate to stand on the penalty spot with a ball. Run out and touch the marker.

As you touch it, your team-mate throws the ball over your head. Step back quickly and leap up.
Try to tip the ball over the bar.

As you step back, turn sideways slightly so that you are facing the ball more.

Index

Cover image © Craig Mercer/Actionplus
Additional designs by Michelle Lawrence
This edition published in 2014 by Usborne Publishing Ltd, 83-85 Saffron Hill, London, EC1N 8RT, England.
www.usborne.com Copyright © 2014 - 1995 Usborne Publishing Ltd.